Talks by a Park Ranger from the

Little Bighorn National Monument

by Gerald Hickman

LitPrime Solutions
East Brunswick Office Evolution
1 Tower Center Boulevard, Ste 1510
East Brunswick, NJ 08816
www.litprime.com
Phone: 1-800-981-9893

Published by LitPrime Solutions: 02/25/2025

ISBN: 979-8-88703-388-4(sc)
ISBN: 979-8-88703-389-1(e)

Library of Congress Control Number: 2024914156

Any people depicted in stock imagery provided by iStock are models, and such images are being used for illustrative purposes only.

Certain stock imagery © iStock.

Because of the dynamic nature of the Internet, any web addresses or links contained in this book may have changed since publication and may no longer be valid. The views expressed in this work are solely those of the author and do not necessarily reflect the views of the publisher, and the publisher hereby disclaims any responsibility for them.

Table of Contents

Little
Indian Encampment
Pony Herd
1
1/2
0
Battle of the Li
Custer
Reno
Benteen
Weir
Native Warriors

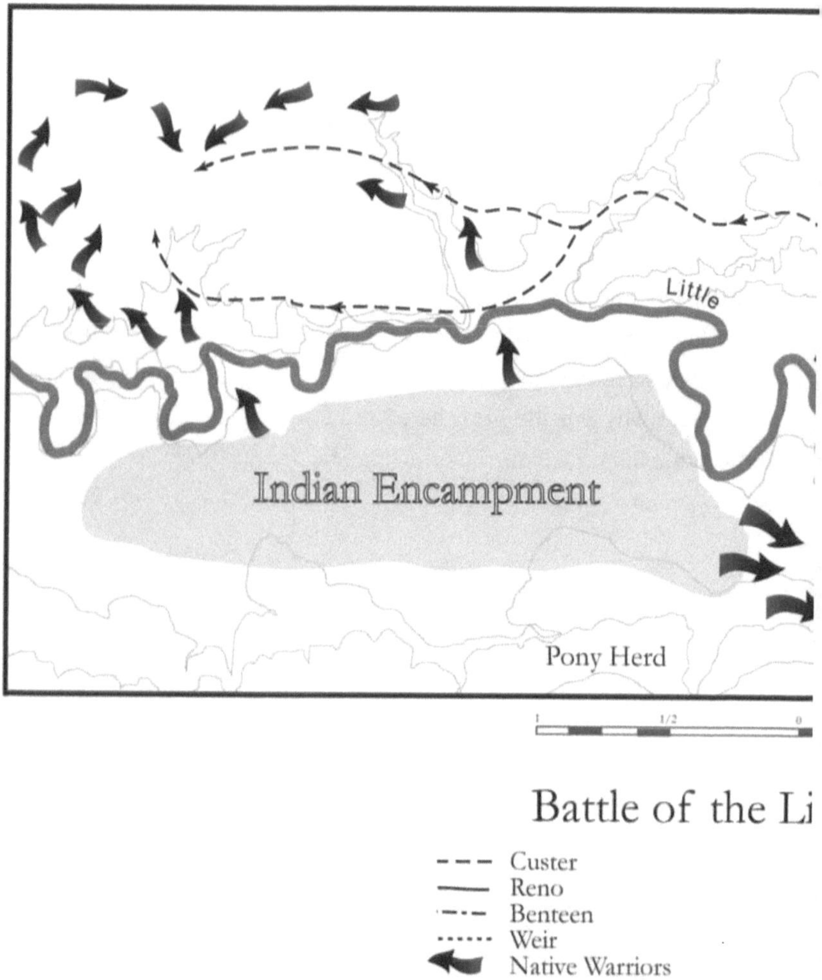

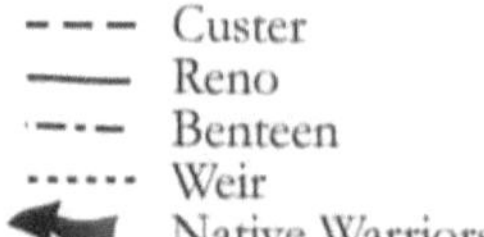

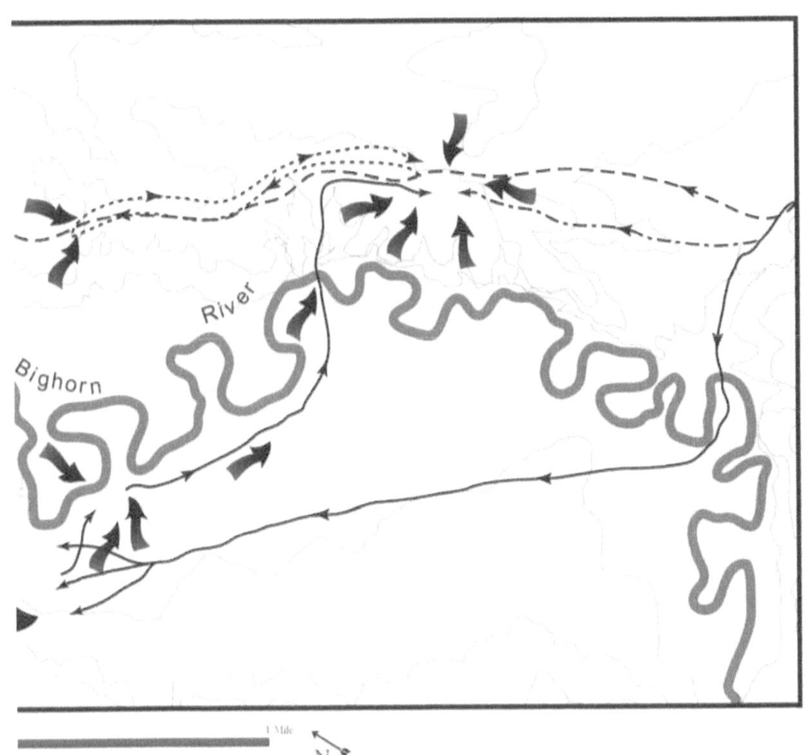

ittle Big Horn

BATTLES BETWEEN INDIAN FORCES
AND U.S. ARMY

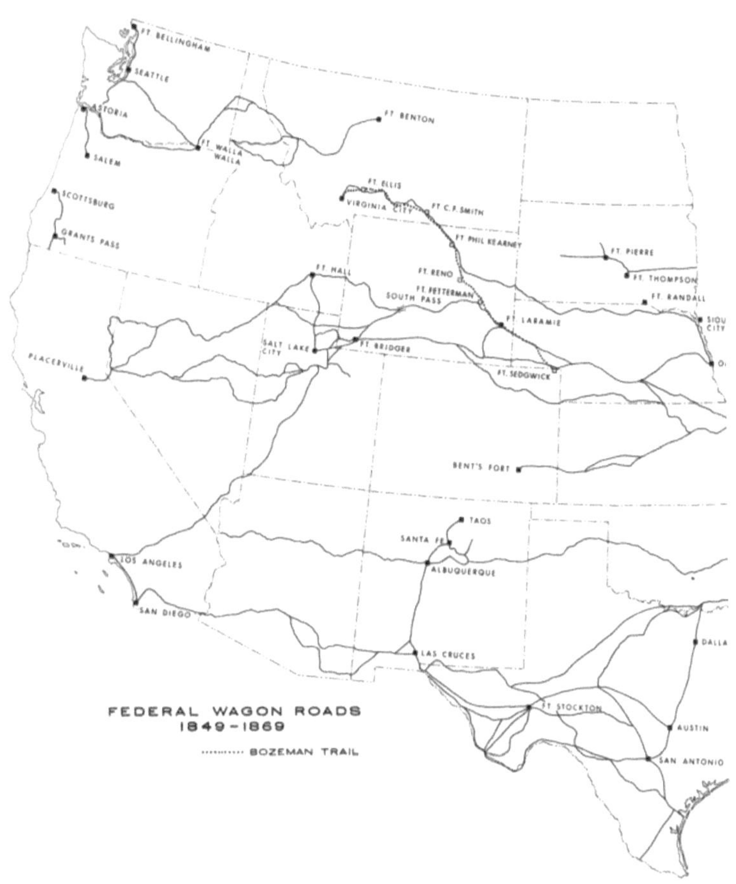

FT. BELLINGHAM
SEATTLE
ASTORIA
SALEM
FT. BENTON
FT. WALLA WALLA
SCOTTSBURG
FT. ELLIS
VIRGINIA CITY
FT. C.P. SMITH
GRANTS PASS
FT. PHIL KEARNEY
FT. PIERRE
FT. HALL
FT. RENO
FT. THOMPSON
FT. FETTERMAN
SOUTH PASS
FT. RANDALL
FT. LARAMIE
SIOUX CITY
SALT LAKE CITY
FT. BRIDGER
PLACERVILLE
FT. SEDGWICK
O
BENT'S FORT
TAOS
SANTA FE
LOS ANGELES
ALBUQUERQUE
SAN DIEGO
DALLA
LAS CRUCES
FT. STOCKTON
AUSTIN
SAN ANTONIO
FEDERAL WAGON ROADS
1849–1869
·········· BOZEMAN TRAIL

TALKS FROM LITTLE BIGHORN

Introduction

I t is a real pleasure and a privilege for anyone to be able to work at the Little Bighorn Battlefield National Monument near Crow Agency in Montana and convey to the visitors what history we know about the fight that took place on the site in 1876. I enjoyed the work and the special feeling that many visitors and Rangers feel for the Greasy Grass and the history of its battle.

The Battle of the Little Bighorn is one of only a few military actions that reflect a significant moment in American history. Another such battle was during the Civil War at Gettysburg, Pennsylvania. Both of these battles represent a turning point in history, both are high water marks in their own right. Currently, over 5,000 books and articles have been published about the Little Bighorn more now than about Gettysburg. George Armstrong Custer was at both of these battles. Without Custer and his volunteer cavalry the turning point of the War could have taken a different direction.

Perhaps Custer's presence was crucial in turning what was a skirmish when compared with many Civil War battles into such a remarkable part of the history of the western frontier. The number of killed in action was small in comparison with major engagements of the War Between the States. However, the significance of the upshot of Little Bighorn on the attitude of the country at large and the determined effort to place all Native Americans on Government established Reservations cannot be minimized. The Battle of the Little Bighorn was the last stand for the buffalo plains tribes.

The Little Bighorn Battlefield National Monument is here to pay homage to warriors, women and children of the Native Americans and to the soldiers who fought and died here. The Battlefield is a special place, mostly unchanged since the day of the fight. This is the only battlefield in the world with markers representing the approximate location of the casualties from the battle. This area is "hallowed ground" with the evidence of a clash between two cultures and an opportunity for the study of history and a chance to experience the feeling of life as a trooper or as a member of the Indian village on the day of the Battle of the Greasy Grass.

Lodges along the Little Bighorn or Greasy Grass River.
Courtesy of the Library of Congress (LOC)

Buffalo Plains Indian Village

For a short period of time in June 1876, a large number of lodges were erected in the valley of the Greasy Grass River These tepees represented the accumulated families of the Lakota or Sioux made up of subtribes including Hunkpapa, Sans Arc, Two Kettle, Blackfoot Sioux, Miniconjou, Brule and Oglala. In addition Lakota allies from the Northern and Southern Cheyenne subtribes were present in the village circle.

There were from 7,000 to 10,000 persons living in this village during the time period when the Battle of the Greasy Grass took place. There were 1,500 to 2,000 fighting men. The horse herd numbered approximately 20,000 animals. There were good numbers of game animals in the area as well. Buffalo were still in the area, with large herds of pronghorn antelope. This valley is a good location for a summer camp because of the abundance of good forage for the herd, firewood and clean water.

Buffalo grazing on the plains of Montana. LOC

The people in this village were a Stone Age culture utilizing what were often considered primitive tools and equipment by the citizens of the United States. The bow and arrow represent the highest level of development in Stone Age technology for the buffalo tribes. The bow was made of ash or osage orange woods either found growing in the area or as trade items from other areas. Arrows were made from chokcherry branches, turkey feathers, buffalo sinew and iron arrowheads. By 1870 few stone or flint arrowheads were being used. The tribesmen could either cut their arrowheads out of a metal object such as a frying pan or barrel hoop or trade bison robes for manufactured arrowheads and other goods.

The source of trade wealth, food, clothing, shelter and tools for the plains culture was the buffalo which roamed the short grass prairie in the millions when Lewis and Clark explored the western portion of the future United States of America. Plains and mountain tribes both hunted the buffalo and used almost every part of the animal in some way or the other. Horn of the buffalo was used to ornament head dresses, for cups and spoons. The buffalo robe with heavy winter hair was as warm as any down sleeping bag of today. Robes from other seasons were used as blankets and rain coats.

Scraping and tanning of buffalo hides to make lodge covers, moccasins and clothing. LOC

Buffalo bones were used as digging tools to harvest vegetable roots used in cooking and medicines. Some tribes who farmed as well as hunting buffalo (like the Mandan tribe who lived along the Missouri River, east of the Little Bighorn River) used many parts of the buffalo in growing food. The hoof, muzzle and hide scrapings of the harvested bison were used to make glue for bow backing, making tools and arrows. Rawhide was used to make ropes, war clubs, parfleche, food containers, clothing bags and shields for battle. The skull was used in ceremonies. Each animal had enough brains to be used to tan the hide of that size animal. Brain tanned leather was a specialty of the Lakota tribe.

One buffalo robe could be traded for many items of various values. Three metal kettles equaled one good quality robe. For ten buffalo robes the warrior could receive a Henry .44 caliber rifle and 100 rounds of ammunition or a muzzleloading trade rifle for eight robes. Other trade goods included steel knives, glass beads from Italy, brass headed nails and copper wire from France, blankets and worsted wool from Great Britain and vermillion dye from China.

Trade with white men was easier for the Crow than some tribes because there were as many as 8 trading posts along the Yellowstone River from 1810 until 1880. But it was still easier to make your own arrows than to have to travel to the Yellowstone every time you shot up all the ammunition for your rim–fire Henry or Winchester 66 rifle. When you used up your quiver full of arrows you made more or traded some buffalo meat to one of the older craftsman in the tribe. Of course, used arrows could be recycled and if the arrow shaft was crooked tools made of buffalo bone could be used to straighten them at night over the fire.

Trade with other tribes and white traders has become a very important enterprise by the middle of the 1800's. In the village, there on the Little Bighorn in June 1876, many tepee covers were made of canvas acquired by trade again for buffalo robes. It would take one woman a year to tan and prepare the number of buffalo hides necessary to make a lodge cover. Often, people decided it more efficient to scrape and tan the buffalo robes for trade and use the lighter and easier to handle canvas covers rather than to use the heavy skin for the lodge covering.

The Indian woman was in charge of the house or tepee. She owned everything in the lodge except the weapons belonging to her husband. If he came home one day and found his belongings outside the front door he was divorced with no lawyer involved and she kept the house. The women and the children could dismantle the lodge, pack it and all belongs on the pack animals and move miles away and be ready to cook dinner when the man came home from hunting with fresh meat for the pot.

General Custer, himself wrote that these people were the greatest light cavalry in the world. They lived outdoors seven days a week and 24 hours each day. They camped out everyday of their lives. In severe weather from over 100 degrees Fahrenheit in the summer to minus 40 degrees Fahrenheit in the winter. The lodge and sweatlodge had evolved over time to be a very good system for survival in a harsh area and a severe environment. Life on the plains would be very different without the horse. The horse was a pack animal and allowed the people to have more goods and a larger lodge. The horse was used as a measure of wealth for the plains tribes but also provided transportation, mobility for war and a vehicle for harvesting buffalo efficiently.

Before the Spanish reintroduced the horse to North America, the plains Indians had used the dog as a beast of burden and a source of food. Lewis and Clark purchased and traded for dog meat from the tribe when game was hard to find on their exploration of the continent. Many tribes used the dog to pack shelter, goods and clothing as they followed the game across the prairie. But with the horse came better times. No longer did the pre-winter hunt depend on a corral technique or a drive over a buffalo jump to secure enough meat to last the whole tribe though a tough winter. The horse allowed greater mobility, carrying more and larger loads of possessions, and the most efficient means of hunting the buffalo.

The horse was an essential component for the buffalo plains tribes' way of life. LOC

There were about 200,000 people living the buffalo culture from the plains of Canada to the deserts of Mexico. Each of these people needed 8 to 10 buffalo per year for food, clothing and shelter plus any tools or weapons made of bison parts. But if you could harvest more animals each year the extra hides could be traded to improve your standard of living. So your wealth was measured, not only by the number of horses in your private herd but by the number of hides and robes you had to offer for trade.

Chapter

2

Cavalry Trooper Circa 1876

The government of the United States had troubles in 1876. The great recession of 1873 was still felt in almost all circles of society in the "States". It was difficult to find work. Especially if you were an immigrant to this country. Young men from Ireland, Germany and Scotland, many of whom could not speak English, had recently moved to the United States.

Discrimination was rampant for many segments of the society and if you were an immigrant especially so. Signs on factories and stores clearly stated, GERMANS AND IRISH NEED NOT APPLY. So, in our countries' history we see not only prejudice against African Americans. Chinese and Native Americans but toward immigrants from Europe as well.

One of the only sources of work for such persons was the US Army in the 1870's. Here was a chance to learn the English language and earn $13 a month while doing so. In 1876 the members of the Seventh Cavalry were 42 per cent foreign born. Of this percentage 19 percent were from Ireland, 17 percent were German, there were also, men from Great Britain (5), Canada, Australia and one from Greece.

One immigrant soldier in the Seventh Cav. was Charles Windolph from Germany. Now one of the reasons Charlie left German was a fear of being drafted. But Charlie had good luck at the Battle of the Little Bighorn because he was with Captain Benteen's troopers. He earned a Medal of Honor at the siege on Reno Hill when he was one of the volunteer marksmen who provided cover fire to protect the water bearers. Charlie survived the battle and lived to be 98 years of age. He died March 11, 1950 and was the longest lived survivor of the soldiers in this engagement. There is a book about Charlie' life, it is called, "I Rode with Custer."

The average age of troopers in this battle was 22. The youngest soldier to die was 17 and the oldest was 56. The rules stated that you had to be 21 to enlist or have parental permission and most frontier enlistments were for 5 years. It was expensive to move men to the frontier so the Army wished to keep them at a frontier post for a reasonable length of time once they were signed up. The average height of a Seventh Cav. fighting man was 5' 7" tall and he could not weigh more than 185 pounds. The idea was to reduce the load for the mounts (which is a term used for the horses). If the soldiers weighed 145 pounds the horse still had another 100 pounds of gear to carry on the front and back of the McClellan saddle.

Re-enactors with authentic uniforms, equipment and horse gear at the Little Bighorn Battlefield National Monument.

Since the average campaign on the frontier was much longer (plus or minus 1000 miles) when compared with the average Civil War campaign (approx. 200 miles), it was necessary in military terms to reduce weight to enable the horses to travel farther and faster on the plains.

Speaking of the War of Northern Aggression or the War Between the States, the nation was sick and tired of fighting and battles and lists of wounded and those killed in battle in the newspapers. And because of these and other reasons, the Army was downsized from over 2 million Union soldiers to about 25,000 to protect the entire frontier by the 1870's. It was not enough men to cover such a large area.

Entertainments on the frontier included: singing groups, raising a vegetable garden (almost every company of soldiers had a garden at Ft. A. Lincoln), performing skits (especially during the winter months), playing cards, gambling, drinking and visiting brothels which were often located near a frontier post.

Some soldiers with a connection to an officer might be able to enjoy hunting or fishing, but such opportunities were limited.

Target practice was not often one of the drills practiced by cavalry troopers in 1876. The US Government in its' wisdom only allowed 8 to 10 cartridges per month for practice, another example of trying to cut back on expenses and save a dollar. With so few cartridges these young enlisted men could barely learn to load and empty their weapon, much less become, a good shot.

Model 1873 "Trapdoor" Rifle, Carbine and Cadet Rifle

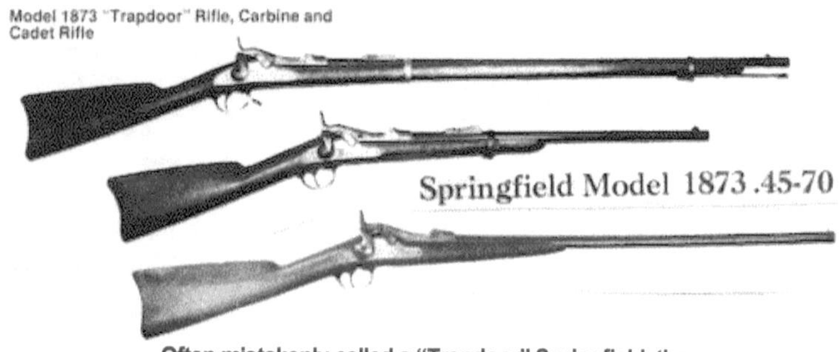

Often mistakenly called a "Trapdoor" Springfield, the .45-55 carbine was the weapon of the Cavalry trooper.

The primary weapon for the trooper was the 1873 model Springfield carbine in .45–55. That is a 45 caliber round with 55 grains of musket powder (that is black powder). The bullet used was a hollow–based .45 caliber weighing 405 grains. The Infantry had the 1873 Springfield Rifle with a 31 inch barrel as opposed to the carbine barrel of 22 inches and the cartridge for the rifle was .45–70. This means the same cal. bullet of 405 grains of lead but fifteen more grains of black powder.

The average trooper or infantry man probably saw fighting only once on average every five years. The life of a soldier on the frontier was one of "glittering misery" as one officer's wife wrote home. There was loneliness, depression, excessive drinking, gambling and problems for enlisted men. The gulf that existed between officer and enlisted men was a wide one. Desertion was a problem and sometimes reached as high as thirty–three percent of the men. When the men were not drilling and training they became slave labor for the Army. So much of a man's enlistment was probably spent at hard labor and not much of it being a soldier.

Chapter

3

Plains lodges in the trees along the stream. LOC

The Little Bighorn Battle

I t was a hot, sultry, windless Sunday that 25th of June, 1876. And it turned out to be one of the bloodiest days in the history of the frontier. Right down in the valley of the Little Bighorn River or the Greasy Grass as it is known to the Buffalo Plains Indians, was the largest village of plains Indians in the history of the USA frontier. Wooden Leg was down in that village, a 17 year old Cheyenne warrior and he said it was the largest village he had ever seen in his life. Black Elk about thirteen winters old in 1876 said there were so many lodges he could not count them all. Black Elk and Wooden Leg both fought in this battle and their narratives along with many others who were there help us to understand what happened that hot, bloody afternoon.

Why were the Indians here?

In my opinion there are three reasons for the presence of this large accidental gathering of buffalo tribesmen:

1. **Religion** Every year a religious ceremony is held in June and in 1876 it was held at Deer Medicine Rocks which is now on the Cheyenne Reservation about 40 miles east of Little Bighorn Battlefield.

2. **Game** There was still good numbers of wild game in the area of the Greasy Grass. The Indian narratives inform us that it was the especially large herds of pronghorn antelope that convinced them to stop and camp in this valley on this trip through the country. The braves went out to hunt and brought back antelope and buffalo while the women set up the lodges and wickiups along the west side of the river north of a large prairie dog town which occupied the valley at this time.

3. **The Notice** During the winter of 1875/76 US President Grant and the Indian commissioners had sent to all winter gatherings a Notice. It said all tribe members must be on their appointed reservation by 31st January, 1876 or the US Army would put the tribes on the appropriate reservation by force if necessary.

Now not all of the men believed the Notice was serious. The Indian Agents had often failed to supply the foods, blankets, trade goods and other items specified in treaties between the Nations and the US Government, the Government had broken many treaties with the various tribes on the plains, and the Great White Father in Washington changed about every 4 years. But if the Government was serious this time, it might be the last summer to live the good life of the old days on the buffalo ranges.

Looking down on the Little Bighorn River from Battle Ridge.

The moccasin telegraph carried messages from the last non–treaty leader of importance, Sitting Bull, to tribesmen still on the various reservations in Dakota and Nebraska territory. "Come out and live the life of the good old days, do not be a slave to the white man's sugar, beef and coffee", he told them. And many reservation residents came out to swell the numbers of the village on the Little Bighorn.

So there are some reasons for the presence of the Lakota and Cheyenne seen by the scouts on the early morning of June 25th.

But...why was the Army here?

Well the Army, especially the Seventh Calvary, was here under orders to place the "hostile tribesmen" back on the hated reservations. The Army did not have orders to come out to the Frontier and shoot all the Lakota and Cheyenne tribe members they could find. Their job was to "round up the hostiles and return them to the appropriate reservation".

A large village of plains Indians. LOC

The best information that the soldiers got from the Indian department of the Government was that the largest possible number of warriors that could be assembled off the reservations was 800. And that these warriors would be found between the Bighorn Mountains on the west and the Powder River area on the east all part of the Crow Indian Tribal Reservation.

The Crow tribe was much smaller than the Lakota and their Cheyenne allies and could not force the large village off their land. Hence, the Crows thought it a good idea to help the Army by scouting and finding the village of hostiles as quickly as possible. The Crows had control of these buffalo hunting grounds since about the time of the Revolutionary War and was officially the stewards of this land since the Treaty of Fort Laramie of 1868. Not only could the Crows help solve this trespass problem by working for the Army as Scouts for $13 a month but they could, also, add to their individual wealth by confiscation of Lakota and Cheyenne horses during or after a fight with hostile tribesmen.

Low Dog, a fighter from the Ogalla of Crazy Horse, said "we were so many, that when I heard the alarm sounded, I thought it was a false alarm, because no one could be so foolish as to attack us in our great numbers". Guess what folks, the US Army was so foolish!

The scouts, guides and interpreters met with Lt. Colonel Custer to tell him about the huge village they hand located. Now many people wonder why we don't refer to Custer as General. Wasn't George Armstrong Custer a General and if so how did he lose his stars? Yes, during the War of Northern Aggression (I can refer to the War Between the States as such because my Great granddad was a soldier in the Confederate Army) Custer was a Brevet Major General of the Volunteer Army. But Custer's rank in the regular Army was Captain during the Civil War. He was promoted to Lt. Colonel when assigned to be the field commander of the newly organized Seventh Cavalry in 1866.

But it was appropriate to refer to Custer by his highest rank earned. He is often called general by his men and others who admired him. He is called by any number of names by those who do not admire him. Custer had graduated from West Point Military Academy second to last in his class.

But for an academic underachiever, he became a popular national figure and hero during his meteoric rise as an officer in the Union Cavalry. From heroic deeds at Gettysburg, when Custer's cavalry defeated Stuart's Confederate horse soldiers, to 17 other victories for the Union, Custer was a source of pride for the Union when many battles were victories for the Confederacy.

Custer's "Luck" was a popular term to help explain his success in the battles of the War Between the States. But along with all the mystery and unknown elements of the fight that took place on the Little Bighorn on the afternoon of the 25th of June, 1876 one thing is for certain, Custer's "Luck" ran out.

Thus it was mid day before the Seventh reached the valley of the Little Bighorn. They found a lone teepee to be used as the burial site for a Sans Arc warrior who had died of his wounds from a fight that Custer knew nothing about. This fight was with General Crook who with over 1000 personnel was one of three Army columns to converge on the hostile tribal members. General Crook was a successful Indian campaigner from the Apache wars in the southwestern deserts and other engagements in California and Oregon. He preferred to ride a mule over a cavalry horse and the Indians knew him as the Gray Fox. One of his old enemies complimented Crook by saying that he never lied to the Indians.

G. A. Custer was the "Boy General" of the Union forces in the War Between the States. LOC

The fight with Crook and his men took place on Rosebud Creek, just about 32 miles from the site of the battle yet to come on the banks of the

Greasy Grass. The date was June 17th, 1876 and it was a hard fight of about 6 hours duration. There was much shooting and charge after charge followed by counter charges. But there were surprisingly few casualties on either the side of the Army under G. Crook or the warriors under Crazy Horse, only about thirty killed or wounded on either side.

But General Crook took his army and 226 Crow and Shoshoni scouts back to Goose Creek (near present day Sheridan, WY) to get more ammunition from his supply depot and to request more soldiers. General Crook had never seen so many fierce fighting warriors in one group before that day on the Rosebud. But this means that Crook will not be available to help the other converging columns of the Army coming from Forts Ellis and Abraham Lincoln from Montana and Dakota Territories respectively.

The really sad thing to tell is that General Crook did not even attempt to send the news of this battle on the Rosebud to the other commanders of this Army campaign. Crook who had never seen such a force of the enemy later said that no messenger could get through to the northern branches of this campaign either Col. Gibbon from Fort Ellis or General Terry in command of this entire campaign from Dakota Territory. General Crook and his men spent the next month fishing and hunting in the Bighorn Mountains while waiting for reinforcements and supplies.

Without information about the number of the enemy to be encountered, General Terry meets Col. Gibbon's column on the Yellowstone River. On June 22nd, 1876, Terry orders the Seventh up Rosebud Creek to locate the hostile bands. This decision was based on the scouting efforts of Major Reno, his battalion and the scouts who had reconnoitered Rosebud Creek drainage from Tongue River June 20 through 22nd. Reno had been a brevet Brigadier General with the Union Army during the War Between the States.

On this scouting mission Reno had taken one Gattling Gun along. But the gun was pulled by condemned cavalry mounts and Rosebud Creek proved too rugged for the fast–firing predecessor of the modern machine gun. The terrain was becoming increasingly more rugged as the Army left the Yellowstone River. The 114 wagons of supplies and forage for the cavalry mounts had to be left at the Yellowstone Supply Depot with the sabers and some other items deemed too heavy for a light, quiet, forced march to the village. Now the Army tried with difficulty to use the untrained wagon mules as pack animals for the rest of the campaign.

When Custer with the entire Seventh, 15 non–combatants, civilians, scouts, guides and interpreters for a total of over 650 souls reached the Lone Tipi, he attempted to capture some of the relatives there mourning the death of the warrior. But they saw the troopers coming and retreated to the large village quickly. This technique worked for Custer on the Washita in 1868 when he captured women and children and the braves surrendered rather than chance shooting near their family members.

Custer's last note says: BENTEEN COME ON BIG VILLAGE BE QUICK BRING PACKS ps. bring packs.

By this time there have been several incidents that could have alerted the large village in the river bottom to the presence of the Army. But for some reason the village is conducting normal activities and sleeping in from several days of celebrating their victory over General Crook at the Battle of the Rosebud. But it still is a mystery to me why the village allows Reno and his men to approach so closely before going out to fight and protect the families in the village. On the 17th the warriors had traveled 32 miles to fight Crook. To me this unknown factor will remain a mystery along with many of the troop movements ordered by General Custer.

Now Custer orders Major Reno to take three companies down the creek bottom and to fight any Indians encountered. Custer promises to support Reno with the fall company. Captain Benteen is sent south to the foothills of the Wolf Mountains to prevent the escape of any peoples to the south and possibly to help protect the pack train which is lagging behind by several miles because of tired, recalcitrant, thirsty mules and horses. Men from all the companies are sent to the rear to help guard the supplies, ammo and equipment as well as the pack animals which are attractive to the Lakota. Of course, the Army does not realize the Indians in the village are as yet unaware of the proximity of the Troops. Ironically, protecting the pack train and carrying messages as ordered by Custer is the salvation of many soldiers who would otherwise have died on Battle Ridge with their regular companions in Custer's battalion.

Reno and Benteen do as ordered. When Major Reno crosses the Little Bighorn River he charges across the flat open ground toward the village. Suddenly, the village awakes to the danger and hundreds of warriors rush out to defend the village. Reno says later that the Indians seemed to grow out of the ground, he halts the charge and forms a skirmish line on the valley floor. Firing at this point is hot for 15 to 20 minutes and bullets from the scouts who have been released by Custer to confiscate horses from the huge herd on the west side of the village or from Reno's men enter the village and accidentally kill women and children.

The Hunkpapa subtribe of Sitting Bull is the southernmost position in the larger village circle and Gall, a young war chief, loses two wives and 3 children early in the battle. Gall who was inspired by the sight of the gray horse troop marching across the bluffs east of the village is now angry and throws down his rifle and promises to fight only with a hatchet for the entire battle. But though he plans to throw away his life this day to join his loved ones, he is not even wounded and lives many years after this fight.

Custer has marched his 210 soldiers north along the bluffs lining the River and from Sharpshooter Ridge he gets a glimpse of the huge village of over 1,000 lodges He sends a messenger back to hurry the pack animals. Sgt. Daniel Kanipe takes a verbal message to Benteen to end his scout to the south and bring up the packs, cutting loose any boxes that slip, but bring those packs.

The troop move down Cedar Coulee into Medicine Tail Coulee, there the commander sends one or two companies down to cross the river and attack the village and thus to support Reno. Custer could see Reno's companies approaching the south end of the village from above on the ridge. At that point it is said, Custer took off his large gray hat waved it and shouted "Harrah boys we have caught them napping".

For apparently many reasons the one or two companies cannot cross at Miniconjou ford except for Private A. Korn whose horse escapes with him on board and races through the village until he can join Reno and his command to the south. More about Private Korn later. Now that Custer has closed with the village he can see what the scouts were trying to tell him at day break: "general, you don't have enough bullets in your whole army to fight that village down there". Now he will try every technique he can to delay because he knows how badly his men will need those packs of 24,000 rounds of ammunition.

Lt. Calhoun and his men are positioned on the south end of Battle Ridge probably to attract the men in the pack train. A skirmish line stretches along Battle Ridge toward Last Stand Hill with men from Capt. Keogh and Lt. Yates companies. After the last messenger leaves Custer no white man lives to tell us what happens to those companies closest to their commander.

But given a summary of Indian battle participant narratives, it now appears that Lt. Col. Custer took about 100 mounted soldiers with him to try to cross the snowmelt swollen river to capture hostages. There was another ford north of the village where the Cheyenne tribes had their lodges near the Oglala sub-tribe of chief Crazy Horse. With the attack by Reno's men to the south of the village, women and children moved to the north of the village to be out of harms reach. Sitting Bull and other older men helped to move and protect these women and children from the Army.

But at this point the Boy General of the Union Army lost his famous luck, because many of the Cheyenne fighting men prevented the Army from crossing the river to the area of the potential hostages. The men with Custer were forced back to the area of the present day National Cemetery by the overwhelming numbers of warriors and the intensity of fire. The skirmishes here cost the lives of 6 soldiers and near the current entrance to the National Monument a soldier and Mark Kellogg's bodies were found days later by Col. Gibbon. Mark Kellogg was the journalist for the Bismarck and New York newspapers and his body could only be identified by the custom boots he wore.

Custer and his remaining men were forced down into the basin just to the east of the National Cemetery. But now the warriors no longer just deployed between the Army personnel and the village. There was now a flanking of the soldiers in the basin and the vast number of warriors was surrounding and cutting off each portion of the Army on Battle Ridge, Calhoun Ridge and in the basin.

Most of the fighting by the Indians was on foot. Only two or so Indian war horses were found dead on the field of battle. The warriors used their weapons very well. About 10 per cent of the warrior had repeating rifles but mostly .44 caliber rimfires which were low power using only about 22 grains of black powder. Another 300 braves used single shot muzzle-loader rifles like trade guns of flintlock and caplock design. But all the warriors had a bow and a quiver of arrows and knew how to use them.

Since four or five winters each young brave had practiced and played with a hand made bow and home made arrows. Games of skill developed instinctive knowledge about the use of this time honored weapon. Hours of play and days of hunting and warfare had made the bow and arrow the weapon of choice for many Cheyenne, Arapaho and Lakota warriors. After all, shoot up all your ammo for a 44 rimfire Henry or Winchester model 66 rifle and you had to go some distance to trade buffalo robes for more ammunition. But use up all your arrows and you could make more or just go pull some out of the last target you hit.

Where the repeating rifle did not penetrate well, the bow could arch a flood of arrows up at an angle to drop behind the breastworks used for protection and hit the soldiers hiding there. The rifle made a lot of smoke and noise but the bow of ash or osage orange was the secret weapon of the Battle of the Little Bighorn for the buffalo plains Indian.

Being in the Basin below the Cemetery and below Last Stand Hill was not the place for a graduate of West Point. Custer was looking for a better defensible position on higher ground. Custer and his men fought their way through to what is now called Last Stand Hill.

Here he gave a command no horse soldier wanted to obey. Shoot your horse and form a breastwork from which to fight. There was a u-shaped line of dead cavalry horses near the top of Last Stand Hill and another line farther down the hill. If you had been there all you could have seen would have been smoke and dust in the still air. Soldiers would have been hunkered behind the bodies of the horses waiting for General Terry and his army coming from the north up on the Yellowstone River and hoping they could get here in time.

The Indian narratives tell us there was so much smoke and dust they could not see the troopers. They just shot arrows and fired their rifles into the smoke in hopes of hitting something. When the soldiers stopped shooting back the warriors rushed in and finished off any wounded troopers.

After the initial battle ended the ritualistic killing and maiming/mutilation of the bodies took place Not all but some Indians believed that in the next world any enemy could come back to haunt you and your family. Thus it was appropriate to mutilate dead enemies to avoid future problems for you and your family. Scalping removed the spirit that was believed to be in the hair. Cutting muscle, fingers or hands prevented the dead from fighting and riding a horse in the next life. Many of these steps were simply insurance to a better life in the spirit world.

The warriors who had defeated Custer's companies now turned their attention to Reno's battalion. When Custer threatened the village many of the braves left Reno's fight in the valley to help protect the village from the new threat to the north. This gave Reno some time to dig in on top of the bluffs east of the village.

The bow and arrow was used successfully at the Battle of the Little Bighorn. Every warrior had a bow and quiver of arrows in addition to other weapons. LOC

The valley fight had been forced into the timber along the river. There for several reasons: such as lack of the anticipated support and Custer's men and need for more ammunition, Reno ordered a retreat to higher ground. Unfortunately, as many as 18 of his men could not hear the order above the din of battle and were cut off in the timber. Most of these men were lucky to survive the fight by hunkering down in the brush and waiting for any opportunity to rejoin the command on the bluffs across the river. And thankfully most of these men survived.

Several of the scouts gave their lives to provide cover fire to allow the trooper to cross the Little Bighorn to the bluffs above. Later these bluffs became known as Reno Hill. Lonesome Charley Reynolds, Stabbed, Isaiah Dorman (the only black man at this battle) and Bob-tailed bull died in the valley with Bloody Knife and Lt. McIntosh.

Once on top of the bluffs a defensive perimeter was established. The soldiers dug in with belt knifes, tin cups and mess kits as well as bare hands. During a lull in the fighting while many warriors were to the north helping to wipe out Custer's men, the men at Reno Hill prepared defenses and Benteen's three companies arrived as did the pack train.

Benteen asked Reno the were-abouts of Custer's command. And Reno ordered him to stay and support this defensive position. Reno was the ranking officer and his order stood. But Capt Thomas Weir had heard the volley fire from farther north and he and his adjutant rode to find the source of the shooting. He was a personal friend of Custer and felt that "soldiers should go to the sound of the shots".

He got as far as what is now called Weir Point before the returning warriors forced all the soldiers back to Reno Hill. Before this ordered withdrawal, Capt. Weir saw through his binoculars Indian riders shooting arrows straight into the ground. He may have witnessed the end of Custer's men on Last Stand Hill.

For over 30 hours Reno, Benteen and Capt. McCollough's packtrain are pinned down on Reno Hill by superior numbers of fighting Indians. A field hospital is established by Dr. Henry Porter in the basin surrounded by the ridges of the defensive perimeter on Reno Hill Dr. Porter is the only one of three doctors originally with this campaign left to treat the wounded. Dr. Porter told the men; "We don't have to wait to be shot men, we all will die without water and soon." Four brave men volunteer to provide cover fire with their Springfield carbines so the water bearers can make several trips to carry water in canteens and camp kettles to help save the wounded. More than a dozen men carry water and only one man is wounded in this effort to save the wounded. His name is Mike Madden an Irish private is hit in the leg. He cannot move, so Half Yellow Face a Crow scout braves enemy fire to carry Mike to the field hospital to Dr. Porter's care, "Mike," Dr. Porter says, "I have to take you leg to save your life." The legend says that the only anesthetic is a bottle of whiskey, so Mike being an Irish man takes a big pull on the bottle. He sighs and says, "Doc if ye give mi anither drink ye cin have mi other leg". Now Mike lived a long life after surviving this battle. He was one of over 350 survivors. And I often wonder if it was his sense of humor or the fact that he drank so much whiskey that helped Mike live so long.

30

TALKS FROM LITTLE BIGHORN

Survivors

Some people jump to the conclusion that there were no survivors of the Battle of the Little Bighorn. But of course most of the Indian combatants lived through the fight on June 25th and 26th, 1876. The exact number of warriors killed in the fight is uncertain but a reasonable figure is between 35 and 70. The warriors were buried quickly after the fight in the draws or along ridges near the battle field by their relatives and tribal friends. A few of the dead were buried in the traditional manner in a lodge left at the village site or on a elevated platform in one of the cottonwood trees along the Greasy Grass River near the village site.

Only a few markers have been placed on the battlefield for the Indian fighters because the exact place where they died is often not well known. The National Park Service goes to great lengths of study and research before placing a marker for anyone who died in the fight along the Greasy Grass River.

Battlefield Marker for Long Road.

Also, the majority of the men with Reno Benteen and the pack train survived. The soldiers buried at the National Monument include the troopers with Custer, civilians and Indian scouts hired by the Army. Several of the Crow Indian scouts released by Custer before his "last stand" took place, lived to older age and are now buried in the National Cemetery at the Little Bighorn Battlefield National Monument. Major Marcus Reno is buried in the National Cemetery at the National Monument along with Curley and Man Afraid of his Horses who were scouts with Custer's men.

The most famous survivor of those with Custer through the end of the battle is the horse, Comanche. This bay horse was the cavalry mount for Captain Miles Keogh who was killed on Battle Ridge to the southeast of Last Stand Hill. Most of the Army horses were taken by the victorious Warriors as trophies of war along with rifles, revolvers and other gear that could be of use to them.

An example of gear useful to the Indian men and women is the high top boots worn by the Cavalry troopers. Indians wear moccasins, and had no use for boots. However, the soft uppers of the high top boots could be cut off the soles and used as containers. And this is why so many cavalry boots soles and heels missing the uppers were found on the battlefield after General Terry and the remainder of the expedition arrived at Last Stand Hill.

But why was Comanche left behind on the field of battle when the other cavalry horses where taken by the tribe members? Some reports indicate that Comanche was wounded and thus left behind with the dead on Battle Ridge. Another idea was that Comanche was anchored to the battle site because the reins were still held in the death grip of Captain Keogh and the Indian people refused to remove the reins from the officer's grip. But for some reason, Comanche was still on the field when the area was secured after the fight.

Comanche was "adopted" by the Seventh Cavalry and lived for years after the battle was over. Private John Korn who was at the battle on Reno Hill was assigned to manage Comanche for the rest of his life. The Seventh Cavalry toured the horse to many of the frontier forts, placed Comanche in many parades and took very good care of him as a reminder of the Indian Conflicts of the Army on the western frontier.

The memories of those Army personnel killed are enhanced by the white markers that can still be seen at Little Bighorn.

White marker for Cavalry Trooper.

When General Terry and Colonel Gibbon arrived at the scene of the battle on June 27th, 1876 the Indian village had been dismantled and the Teton Sioux, Cheyenne and other tribes had departed. All the fallen warriors had been removed for traditional burial before the Army arrived on June 27th, 1876.

As the burial parities from the Army buried the fallen white men a stake was driven into the ground where the body was found. If the identity of the individual could be determined by friends or army acquaintances, the name of the soldier was attached to the stake.

This is one of the very few battlefields in the world where names and identities of fighters are located where they fell. It is a stirring sight to witness the red stone markers for Indian fighters and white markers for soldiers on the hills and ridges of this battlefield in the prairie country of modern-day Montana.

The Indian Memorial was dedicated in June, 2003.

Index

Photo Credits: Photographs labeled "LOC" are courtesy of the Photo & Print Catalog at the Library of Congress and reproduced here for educational purposes with their written consent. The rest of the photos were taken by Gerald Hickman and Shannon Hickman.